Graphic design and illustrations: Zapp

© 1995 Tormont Publications Inc.
338 Saint Antoine St. East
Montreal, Canada H2Y 1A3
Tel. (514) 954-1441
Fax (514) 954-5086

ISBN 2-89429-697-5

Printed in China

BEAUTY AND THE BEAST

TORMONT

Once upon a time, there was a rich merchant who had three daughters. The two older girls were bad-tempered and selfish. But the youngest, Beauty, was gentle and kind.

$\mathcal{O}$ne day, the merchant's ships were all lost in a storm. Suddenly, he was poor. He had to move his family to a small farm in the country.

The two older sisters complained all day because they no longer had fancy dresses or servants. But Beauty did the chores, and tried to make a cheerful home.

$\mathcal{T}$hen one day, a messenger arrived
with news. One of the merchant's ships
had survived the storm after all! The
merchant set off at once to see if any of
his fortune remained.

"Bring us the latest dresses from
Paris," the two older sisters said.

"And what would you like, Beauty?"
he asked.

"I would love a rose, Papa. We don't
have any in our garden," Beauty said.

"A rose for my Beauty," he promised.

But when the merchant arrived at the port, he discovered that all his cargo had washed overboard in the storm.

Broken in spirit, he set out for home. But on the way, he got caught in a terrible snowstorm. He couldn't see where he was going and soon realized he was lost.

$\mathcal{J}$ust when he had given up all hope of finding his way home, he spied a light in the distance. He followed the light down a long avenue of trees. At the end of the avenue was a house so magnificent that it resembled a palace.

*H*e found a stable for his horse, and then walked toward the great house. The doors swung open as if he were expected.

"Hello? Is anyone home?" he called out several times. But there was no reply.

The merchant entered a room with a
blazing fire. A grand meal was laid out for
one person. At first he hesitated to help
himself, but he was so cold and hungry, he
finally sat down and ate to his heart's
content.

$\mathcal{F}$eeling braver after his meal, the merchant explored the house. He soon found a bedroom. The bedcover was turned down, all ready for someone. Gratefully, he sank onto the bed and was soon fast asleep.

In the morning, he found his clothes neatly pressed, and a new cloak. A hearty breakfast was waiting for him. "What wondrous magic is this," he sighed as he finished his meal.

He could find no one to thank for his stay, so he headed for the stable. On the way, he came upon a beautiful rosebush.

"Well, at least Beauty shall have her wish," he thought. But as soon as he plucked a rose, he heard an awful roar behind him.

The merchant turned around to see a huge beast step from behind the trees.

"It isn't enough that I feed and clothe you," the beast roared. "But now you steal from me!"

"Forgive me, my lord...!" the merchant pleaded.

"...My lord indeed," the creature replied. "Do you not see that I am a beast? My name is Beast!"

"The rose was for my youngest daughter,"
pleaded the merchant, trembling.

"Then I will spare your life if you
promise that one of your daughters shall
come and live here willingly," snarled the
Beast. The terrified man promised, adding
that if none of his daughters would agree,
he himself would come back to die.

The merchant went home sadly and
told his daughters of his terrible promise.
Before the other sisters could speak,
Beauty offered to go.

*W*hen Beauty and her father arrived at the great house, it was empty, as before. But this time, a mouth-watering meal was set for two. Halfway through their meal, they were startled by the sudden appearance of the Beast.

"Do you come here willingly?" he asked Beauty.

"Yes, I do," she replied softly.

"Good," the Beast said. "You may spend a last evening with your father, but when he leaves tomorrow he must never return. You will only be able to see him through the magic mirror in your bedroom, but that is all." Then the Beast disappeared before either of them could say a word.

Beauty and her father found their rooms and sadly said goodnight.

That night, Beauty dreamed that a lovely lady stood by her bed. "Do not be sad, Beauty. Your selfless act will be rewarded, and all who love you will be well," the lady whispered.

The next morning, Beauty kissed her father goodbye. "Do not despair, Papa," she said. "I had a wonderful dream last night. I know I will be safe here. Everything will be all right."

$\mathscr{B}$eauty missed her father terribly, but she found ways to enjoy herself. The huge house was full of wonderful paintings, and there were gardens filled with exotic flowers and birds. There was a library, and a music room.

Beast joined her every evening for dinner, and Beauty soon got used to him.

$\mathcal{W}$henever they were together, he was gentle and amusing. "Are you still afraid of me?" asked the Beast one evening.

"No, Beast, I'm not afraid," she smiled.

"Then will you marry me?"

"Oh, I could never *marry* you!" she gasped, taken completely by surprise.

After that, the Beast avoided Beauty until, one day, he appeared in the garden. "You look sad. Why is that?" he asked.

"I saw my father in the magic mirror. He's ill. Please let me go to him," she pleaded.

The Beast looked sad. Finally, he slipped a ring onto her finger. "Wear this tonight, and take it off when you wish to return. But if you stay longer than a week, I will surely die."

Next morning, Beauty awoke in her father's home.

Beauty nursed her father back to
health, and did not notice the days
fly by. Too late, she remembered her
promise! Quickly, she kissed her father
goodbye and slipped the ring off her
finger.

Instantly, she was back in the
palace. She searched everywhere, but
she couldn't find the Beast. Dinner was
served, but his chair remained empty.
She was too upset to eat, and stepped
out into the garden. As she did so, she
heard a low moan beside the fountain.
It was the Beast!

"Dearest Beast!" cried Beauty,
running to him. She lifted his head
onto her lap. "You're ill, and it's all
my fault!"

"*B*eauty, you broke your promise, and now I'm dying," the Beast groaned.

"You mustn't die!" sobbed Beauty. "I realize now how much you mean to me. I love you and would gladly marry you." As she spoke, her tears fell on the Beast's face.

Suddenly a wonderful thing happened. The Beast faded away, and in his place rose a handsome prince.

"Where's Beast?" cried Beauty in confusion.

"I am Beast," replied the Prince. "You have broken a terrible spell. I was doomed to remain a beast until a true heart could love me for myself and wish to marry me."

Then, as if by magic, the lovely lady of Beauty's dreams came up to them. She was really the Prince's mother, and with her were Beauty's father and sisters.

And so Beauty and the Prince were married, and lived happily all the days of their lives.